FACING YOUR FEARS

FACING YOUR FEAR OF SHOTS

BY HEATHER E. SCHWARTZ

Consultant:
Tawnya M. Ward, PsyD, LP
Clinical Psychologist
Shakopee, Minnesota

PEBBLE
a capstone imprint

Published by Pebble, an imprint of Capstone.
1710 Roe Crest Drive, North Mankato, Minnesota 56003
capstonepub.com

Copyright © 2023 by Capstone. All rights reserved. No part of this publication may be reproduced in whole or in part, or stored in a retrieval system, or transmitted in any form or by any means, electronic, mechanical, photocopying, recording, or otherwise, without written permission of the publisher.

Library of Congress Cataloging-in-Publication Data is available on the Library of Congress website.
ISBN: 9781666355505 (hardcover)
ISBN: 9781666355567 (paperback)
ISBN: 9781666355628 (ebook PDF)

Summary: Explores the reasons why many people are afraid of shots and provides simple tips for facing this fear safely.

Editorial Credits
Editor: Donald Lemke; Designers: Sarah Bennett and Jenny Bergstrom; Media Researcher: Julie De Adder; Production Specialist: Katy LaVigne

Image Credits
Getty Images: Dejan Dundjerski, 5, FatCamera, 15, JGI/Tom Grill, 18, omgimages, 19, SDI Productions, cover, 9, 13, Sean Justice, 12, ViewStock, 14; Shutterstock: Davizro Photography, 10, Domira (background), cover and throughout, Kapitosh (cloud), cover and throughout, Marish (brave girl), cover and throughout, Monkey Business Images, 4, New Africa, 8, Olena Yakobchuk, 17, paulaphoto, 11, Peakstock, 21, photastic, 20, Prostock-studio, 16, TinnaPong, 7

All internet sites appearing in back matter were available and accurate when this book was sent
to press.

Printed and bound in the USA. 4882

TABLE OF CONTENTS

Scared of Shots 4

All About Shots 6

Needles Are Needed 10

After a Shot 16

    Help a Fuzzy Friend 20

    Glossary 22

    Read More 23

    Internet Sites 23

    Index 24

    About the Author 24

Words in **bold** are in the glossary.

SCARED OF SHOTS

A lot of kids fear going to the doctor for one reason. They don't like shots. Just the idea of getting a shot might make you worry.

But shots are important. Learning more about them can help you feel calmer at the doctor's office.

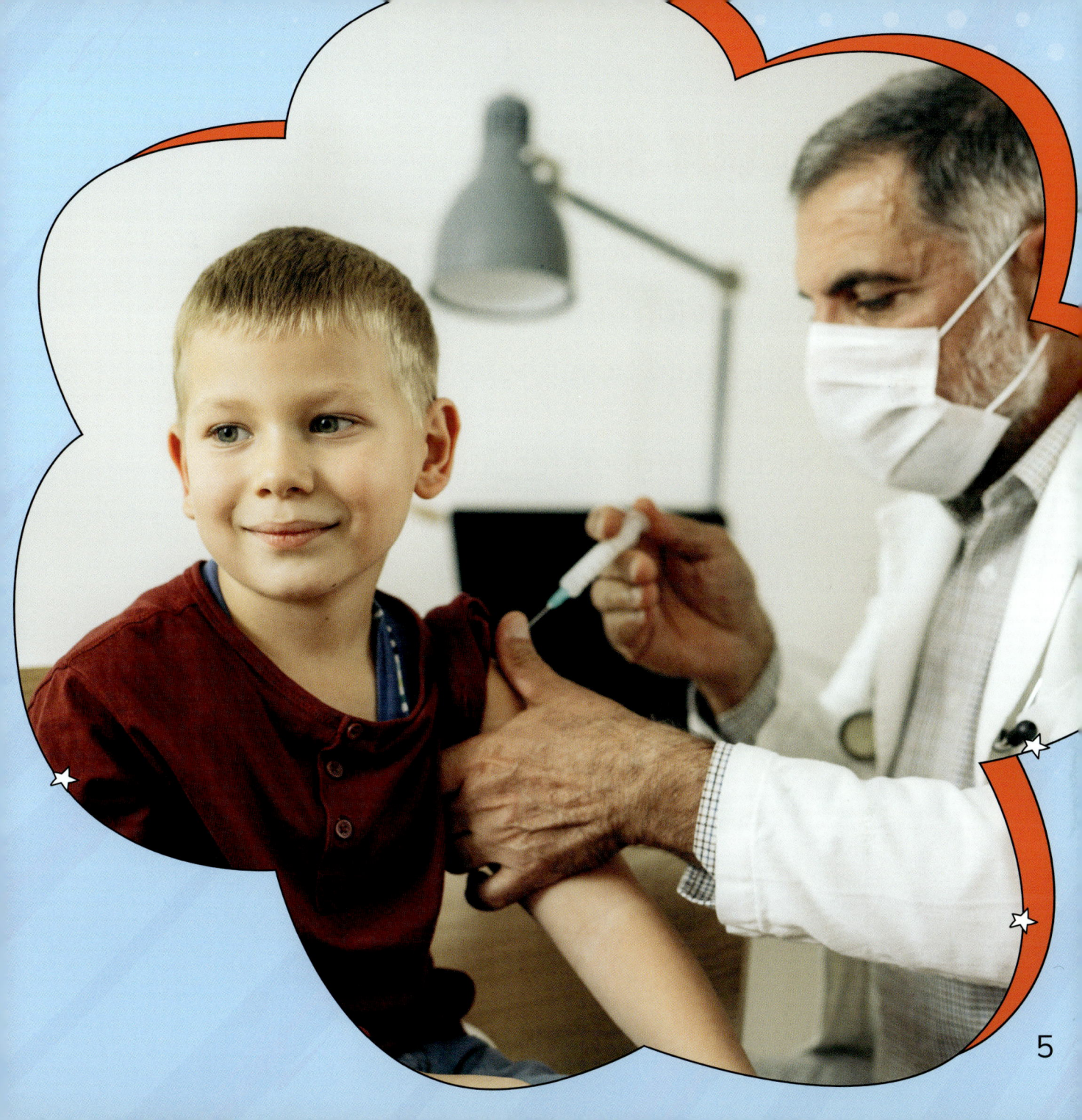

ALL ABOUT SHOTS

Do you ever wish shots didn't exist? Then you wouldn't have to think about them. You would never have to get them.

But shots are good for you. They help keep you healthy. They teach your body how to fight **illnesses**.

Shots can deliver **vaccines**. Vaccines teach your body how to fight diseases. Some vaccines do this by using a weak or dead virus that won't make you sick.

After a vaccine, your body knows how to fight the virus. Your **immune system** can beat the disease and keep you well.

NEEDLES ARE NEEDED

Shots get into your body through a needle. Some people dislike needles. But not everyone does. You don't have to be afraid just because other people feel fearful.

Try this trick to calm down. Ask yourself: "Am I scared of needles?" Maybe the answer will surprise you. Maybe you are not afraid of them.

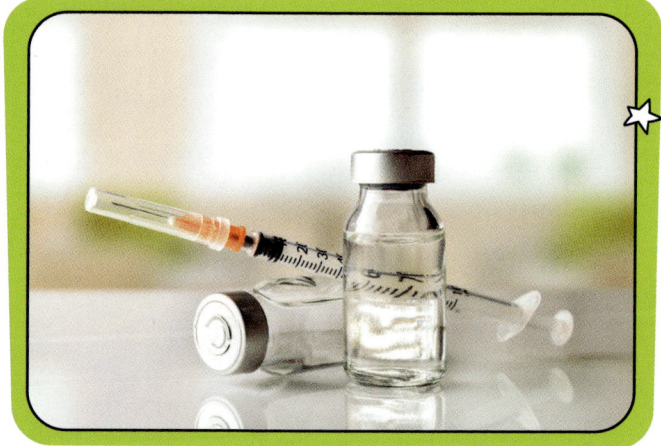

Shots are easier to handle if you can relax. One way to do that is by not thinking about them.

☆ When it's time for a shot, focus your mind on a happy memory. **Distract** yourself by singing a song. Try telling a joke to the nurse.

Some people do not like seeing the needle when they get a shot. You do not have to watch. You can look away. You can close your eyes. You never see the needle at all!

Being surprised by a shot is not pleasant either. Don't be afraid to speak up. Tell the nurse if you want to know exactly when it's going to happen.

AFTER A SHOT

After a shot, your arm might feel **sore**. You might have **side effects**, such as a fever. This does not mean that you have an illness. You will feel better soon.

Tell an adult if you don't feel well. Rest and medicine can help.

Getting a shot is not very fun. You probably won't ever learn to like it. But you can relax and get through it. Remind yourself that shots are over in a flash.

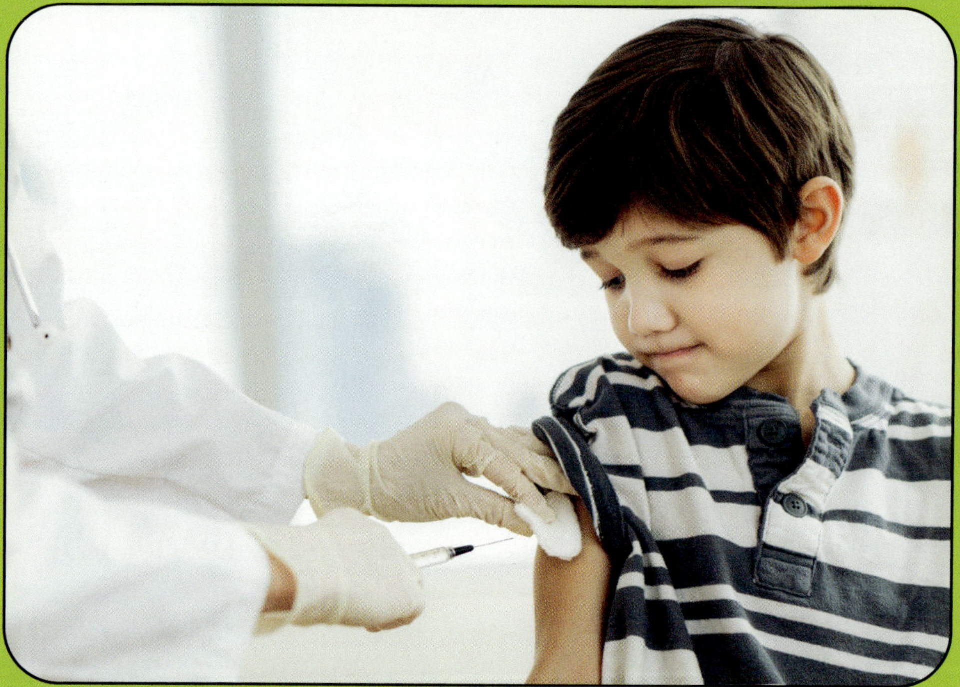

Remember how helpful shots can be. They protect you and others around you from illness. That way, you can stay well and have some real fun!

HELP A FUZZY FRIEND

Pretend you are taking a stuffed animal to the doctor for a shot. Your stuffie is scared. How can you help your fuzzy friend feel better?

What You Need

- paper
- pencil
- stuffed animal

What You Do

1. Think of one idea to relax before a shot.
2. Think of one idea to stay calm during a shot.
3. Think of one idea to feel better after a shot.
4. Write down all of your ideas.
5. Practice these ideas with your stuffed animal.
6. Then put your list of ideas in a safe place. Look at it the next time you need a shot!

GLOSSARY

distract (dis-TRAKT)—to draw attention away from something

illness (IHL-nuss)—a condition of being unhealthy in your body or mind

immune system (uh_MYOON SIS-tuhm)—the system that protects your body from illness, infections, and disease

side effect (SYDE uh-FEKT)—an unwanted effect of a drug or chemical that occurs along with a desired effect

sore (SOR)—painful

vaccine (vak-SEEN)—a substance that is usually injected into a person to protect against a particular disease

READ MORE

Hoena, Blake, A. *A Visit to the Doctor's Office.* North Mankato, MN: Capstone, 2018.

Klepeis, Alicia Z. *Super Science Feats: Medical Breakthroughs Vaccines.* Minneapolis: Jump! Inc.: 2021.

Sisteré, Mariona Tolosa, and Ellas Educan Collective. *The Secret Life of Viruses.* Naperville, Illinois: Sourcebooks eXplore, 2021.

INTERNET SITES

Nemours KidsHealth: A Kid's Guide to Shots
kidshealth.org/en/kids/guide-shots.html

Nemours KidsHealth: Kids Talk About: Feeling Scared
kidshealth.org/en/kids/comments-scared.html

PBS Kids: A Visit to the Doctor: Daniel Tiger's Neighborhood Videos
pbskids.org/video/daniel-tigers-neighborhood/2260372863

INDEX

doctors, 4

feeling sick, 16

illness, 6, 8, 16, 19

medicine, 16

needles, 10, 14

nurses, 13, 15

pain, 16

relaxing, 12, 18

staying calm, 4, 10,

vaccines, 8

ABOUT THE AUTHOR

photo by Dan Doyle

Heather E. Schwartz has written hundreds of children's books. She lives in upstate New York with her husband, two kids, and two cats named Stampy and Squid. She often laughs when she feels scared, which helps her calm down.